Second Son

Ian Alexander

Second Son

Second Son
ISBN 978 1 74027 455 5
Copyright © text Ian Alexander 2007

First published 2007
Reprinted 2017

GINNINDERRA PRESS

PO Box 3461 Port Adelaide SA 5015
www.ginninderrapress.com.au

Contents

1. My brother's father

I've got the stigmata again: that itching blister of guilt on my sinless palms. No one but me knows why I get these God-marks on my hands, and scratching only opens up old wounds. We were there, Mary and I, and we watched them nail him up, but now Mary is dead, and beyond good and evil. Her innocence need trouble her no longer, but mine bubbles up like plague boils now she is gone.

What is truth? The truth is this: I never killed a man, and I never lied. I have done nothing to deserve all this: no one can claim that it is because of me that Jerusalem burns, no one has the right to throw me overboard to save the threatened ship of God's kingdom. I never fought or struggled in the street, I never spat at a soldier, I never lit a signal fire in the night, or crossed swords and breathed bloody oaths with traitors. I never raised my fist and shouted 'freedom', because I never believed that freedom was a thing to be won from others. Does a sick man strive against an enemy in order to be well? If he burns the house of a healthy man, will his disease leave him?

I lived, for the most part, a quiet and blameless life: I never lied, I never killed a man, and the only wife I coveted was mine. To the people in this camp I would be just one more old man compelled to proclaim his innocence – the compulsion itself sufficient proof of guilt – but I know from forty years of experience that the only cure for these sores is to tell that dreadful story once again. Because my Mary is dead, and cannot hear me (though I stroke her dear head as I write) and because the world at large believes it knows my story before I start to tell it, so this pen and these pages will have to take the place of tongue and ears, and I will deal with the past alone. The past, and my brother, alone.

I am a carpenter, and my father was a carpenter, but I have no idea who my brother's father was. What should I believe? That almighty God slept with my mother? My mother never held this to be true, and I find it hard to call her a liar. I am not strong in faith. I don't know. In any case, my brother thought he was different from the rest of us. Different from James, different from John, different from our sisters, and different, most of all, from me. Of all of us it was he and I who looked most alike, but it was never hard to tell us apart, because his face glowed like a lamp, whereas mine always seemed to threaten rain. Everyone who looked at Jesus's face believed they saw love flowing out of him: enough to fill the whole world with love. In a way it was true. He loved the world and all the people in it, but he wasn't very good at loving actual individual people, one at a time. Few knew him well enough to realise that, but I knew it and my wife came to know it. Few got close enough to feel how cold he was. Those who saw him preach and heal, who knew him only as a public figure, remember only his overflowing love. Clearly it was hard to hate my brother. That, I suppose, was my special gift.

We grew up surrounded by God and by talk of God; they made him seem almost a solid thing, but faith was not an art I ever mastered. I could never learn to believe. I was a simple, direct man: an earthly man, if not a worldly one. I knew wood, I knew sheep and fish, I knew stones and crops and houses: God was something I could never grasp. When Jesus and I laboured side by side in my father's workshop, I respected the wood as a thing in itself. I strove to bring the best table, the best door out of the wood I had. It was a tricky, knotty, material thing, and it was the challenge of my trade to master it and shape it to useful ends.

Jesus never felt this way: his kingdom was not of this world. Does this make him a prophet? It made him a lousy carpenter. My beds squatted firmly on the floor; his squeaked and rocked no matter how many were sleeping in them. If God created this world – which is, above and in spite of all things, an awesome and beautiful place – then how could his only son so far fail to reflect his skill? If my brother had built that cross they nailed him to, it would have fallen apart in his hands.

One of us must have been wrong. Either he failed to appreciate the solid presence of the wood, or I failed to feel its spirit. To me a piece of wood was just a thing, a tree-no-longer, but he saw it primarily as a gift, or a dream, or a manifestation of God. He grieved for the tree in a way I never could. I loved trees. I could climb them, sit in their shade, eat their fruit, and build useful things from their wood, but Jesus loved them above all the uses he could find for them: more the way I loved people. He would ask permission before he plucked a fig, thank the tree personally for its shade, apologise before he picked up a saw, and then consign to the flames of hell living people who he had never met, simply for the sake of their beliefs. I could never learn to believe in a god that had a son like that.

But it was only later that I noticed these things: looking back, it seems that the first hint we had that there was something unusual about my brother was when he was twelve. I am ignoring the stories about angels announcing his imminent conception and his birth, supposedly wise men bringing him absurdly symbolic gifts, and ludicrous genealogies which trip over each other in an attempt to demonstrate that my humble father – to whom my brother was apparently unrelated – was the descendant of King David, in whose city a spurious census enabled my brother to be born. No, the first clue that we were dealing with anything out of the ordinary came when we were on our way home from Jerusalem after the Passover festival. Most of us couldn't wait to leave that ugly, dusty land and get back to Galilee, where at least the trees didn't look as if they had to fight the devil to raise their heads above the ground, but Jesus wanted to stay. That was the clue: not the details of what he may or may not have said in conversation with the scribes, but the fact that he loved Jerusalem. He loved it, and he wanted one. The typical Galilean finds it hard to imagine that any sensible god would want to build his holy city on a dusty, rocky hill, but my older brother had no such typical feelings: he wanted to stay, so he sneaked away from the group and went back to the temple.

I had seen him turn back and head for the city, but I kept my mouth shut and hoped that no one else would notice. I was only eleven myself, and young enough to think that once my parents realised that Jesus was gone, they would simply say, 'Oh well, now Judas is the oldest son.' Far from it. Of course we had to leave the band we were travelling with and turn back. We had to retrace our steps until we came to the gates of Jerusalem, and we had to search the city until we found my idiot brother. And there he was, sitting in one of the lesser courtyards of the temple, surrounded by an indulgent group of scribes who were clearly amused by this boy who talked – even then – in puns and spurious analogies. There was little in the adult Jesus's words to distinguish them from the shrill, precocious boy who sat there lapping up the attention. When he saw us, sweaty and dusty after our fruitless day's walk, he made that unbearably smug comment about a shepherd who loses one sheep being happier to find it than he is about the ninety-nine which never got lost. I knew shepherds, so I knew that what he was saying was rubbish, and when my mother strode over to where he sat, I thought for a delicious moment that she was going to slap his face, but instead she picked him up and hugged him. And it was then I learned that what is false and stupid when spoken of shepherds may even so be true of parents, and that was my brother's strength: if you looked closely at his words they came apart before your eyes, but they left such a powerful impression that they seemed true anyway. To others.

So yes, the old man with the itching palms is Judas, and if you have heard of me you already hate me, but what you have heard is hardly true. Think who you heard it from. You have heard of silver pieces, of remorse, of the various ways in which others wished that I had died. You have heard my name used as a curse, as if the very word meant traitor, but even that no longer hurts me. I have lived too long for that.

My brother's followers have argued that I betrayed him, but I will argue otherwise: I will argue that the last thing he needed was followers.

From the moment he came back from the desert, they followed him. He crossed the lake and they followed him. He went up to the mountains and they followed him. He hid in the wilderness and sought out every obscure place, but everywhere they followed him and told others to follow him.

He insulted their laws and slandered their customs, and they followed him. He spat on their ancestors and turned their loved ones against them, and they followed him. He promised them obscurity, injury, poverty and death, but still they followed him and called themselves his followers, and made outrageous claims on his behalf.

Because they wished to follow, they called him leader. Because they lacked wisdom, they called him teacher. Because they were sheep, they called him shepherd, when they should have called him wolf.

So he went to Jerusalem and they followed him, and waved palm fronds at him and stole donkeys for him. So he defiled their temple and blasphemed their god, and though they kept their distance and denied they ever knew him, still they followed. And when finally he was taken to the place of the skull and nailed to a piece of wood and left to breathe his last, there also they followed him and watched him.

He crossed over into death and thought he was beyond their following, but even in his tomb they would not let him rest. He said, 'Where I am going you cannot follow', but they did. Oh, in their thousands they followed him there, the fools.

2. The heavens torn apart

We went down to the Jordan to see the madman John baptising the repentant: excess of piety has always been a great tourist attraction for our people, especially in dark times. He was a sight. I am glad that no one had yet invented the idea that we were cousins. He was tall and very thin, his beard was tangled and wispy, and when he bent his head towards the ground we could see that he was on the way to baldness. His nose was like a beak, and his eyes never rested anywhere quite long enough. He seemed to be a man at the very limit of his patience, kept waiting for his loved one so far beyond his endurance that when she arrived he would tear her to pieces.

I assumed at the time that the beloved who had kept him in this state was salvation, or some other theological abstraction, but as it happened it was my brother. That is a strange feeling. John was a gutter prophet with a gutter prophet's way of mangling other people's words and claiming that they were soon to be fulfilled: Isaiah and the Psalms seemed to be his favourites. He was making a straight path for the Messiah; he was making mountains into level plains; he was preparing the way of the Lord, whose sandals he was not worthy to untie, and so on. It was all pretty amusing to a simple carpenter who had as much expectation of the Messiah as he did of marrying the high priest's daughter, but I looked across at Jesus and I saw that he was getting that odd, distant look in his eyes which usually came over him just before he hit his thumb with the hammer. Except that this time it was focused on the crazed stranger in the river, and Jesus was climbing down the river bank to join him, and John was making loud proclamations over my brother's head and declaring that his wait was over: here was the salvation of Israel, here was the Lord's anointed, here was the one whose sandals he was not worthy to untie. I looked down at my sandals, which were, in fact, identical to his, both pairs having been made by old Bartholomew in Nazareth.

But then John grabbed my brother's nose and thrust his head into the water to wash his sins away, and when Jesus was thoroughly baptised and trying to regain his breath, he saw the heavens torn apart and the Spirit descending on him, and a voice spoke to him from heaven saying, 'You are my son, my beloved, the chosen one who I have made in my image in order to do my work among my people on earth', and the Spirit drove him out into the desert and for forty days put him to the test. That's what he saw, but I can't vouch for anyone else. I saw my brother gasping for breath, dripping muddy water, looking like the victim of a practical joke, but he saw doves and heard voices and wandered off into the desert.

A little conjecture is required to fill in what happened next, and this story which I imagine is all based on hints and clues and muttered comments around campfires, but it seems to me that a man can only be tempted by the things in his head, and I think I know the contents of my brother's head better than most.

So picture Jesus in the desert, ill-prepared, not having eaten, becoming very hungry, and the Spirit testing him, tempting him, teasing him, licking soft and honey words in his dry ears, saying, 'If you wish to eat, my son, then command these stones to become bread and end your hunger, for is there any reason why these stones should not become bread, or why you should not eat stones themselves, or why one loaf should not become five thousand, or you yourself become a loaf or a stone? You have this power: you are the bread of life; you are the cornerstone of the new temple. Simply demand this day your daily bread, and what you need you will have, for who would give his child a stone who asked for bread, or a snake who asked for fish? Not I. Do you not remember how King David and his companions, being hungry, ate the consecrated loaves that only the priests may lawfully eat? Then let the one who is without sin eat the first stone.'

But Jesus refused to satisfy his hunger, and replied, 'The son of man shall not live by bread and stones, but by every word from the mouth of God.'

Then the Spirit took him to the top of a mountain and showed him all the nations of the world and every form of power and wealth and honour and luxury: buildings covered with gold and glass, with domes and spires pointing to heaven, robed choirs singing sacred hymns, worldly authority and spiritual might, and one thousand years of rule under his unchallenged name. And when he had shown and described all these things, he said to Jesus, 'I will give you all of this if you will bow down and worship me. All power in heaven and earth will be granted to you: what you bind on earth will be bound in heaven, and what you loose on earth will be loosed in heaven. You will pick up serpents and not be harmed, walk on hot coals and not be burned, and death will have no hold on you. You will walk on water and calm the storm with your voice. You will give sight to the blind, strength to the lame and speech to the mute. At your word, demons will cast themselves out and exalt your name, trees will wither, mountains will be flung into the sea, and the dead will return to life. Simply worship me and your name will be known to the ends of the earth; worship me and your followers will go out and make disciples of every nation; bow down and worship me and all these things will come to pass, that at the name of Jesus every knee shall bow and every tongue confess you Lord. Come with me, and I will make you a fisher of men.'

But Jesus was not swayed by what he was offered, and replied, 'Scripture says to worship God and serve him only.'

Finally the Spirit took him to the highest point of the temple and sang him a lament, saying 'Behold Jerusalem. Have you not longed to gather up her children as a hen gathers her brood, yet they refused to hear you? Though they are like sheep without a shepherd, you will find no faith in them. This faithless and perverse generation: how long will you be with them? How much longer can you put up with them? Can they drink the cup that you must drink? Have they the strength to stay awake with you for one hour? Will they not disown you and forsake you and run away? Is not your soul sorrowful to the point of death? Sleep now and have your rest: it is all over. Hurl yourself down from here, for will not God send twelve legions of angels to catch you up to the throne of heaven in the blinking of an eye?'

Then Jesus raised his head and said, 'Scripture says not to put God to the test', but the Spirit turned from him and said, 'Whose son is this? Away from me, you evil one. You think only of yourself, not of God: it is for this moment that you have come. Greater love has no man than to lay down his life for his friends.'

Then the Spirit left him once more and he found himself in a dry and rocky place. He repented of all the things he had said, and he wept: the voice of one who cries in the desert.

3. Today these words can be erased

It was early in the month of Heshvan when Jesus returned. The wheat and grapes were in, and the year was slipping mildly into winter, when we heard that he was down in the synagogue, preaching. My brothers and I cringed at the thought of him shaming us in front of our pious neighbours, so we went to bring him home.

When we saw him, we realised that he had not been having a peaceful time since he left us on the riverbank: his face was like dried beef, and he was clearly out of his mind. I learned in that moment what happens to people who consort with spirits: the soft, vague ascetic who couldn't drive a nail had somehow become a hard, scrawny prophet with eyes that could tell nails to drive themselves. His eyes were the maddest things I had ever seen: if they condemned you to hell, you would need the will-power of a mountain to go anywhere else. You spend time with spirits, you end up looking like one: I can't think of a better reason for having nothing to do with them. So explain this to me: why did I follow him? Why did I leave my home and my workshop and my mother and follow him? Tell me that.

He was standing there in the synagogue with the fifth scroll of the Law in his hand, and he found the place he wanted and read to them:

> If anyone has a son who remains stubborn and rebellious, even though his parents punish him, you must seize him and take him before the elders at the town gate and say to them, 'This son of ours remains stubborn and rebellious, even though we punish him: he is a liar and a drunkard and a slut.' All the people must then stone him to death. You must banish this evil from among you.

This was the first time he had preached – the first time he had raised his voice in public – and in retrospect it would have to be called the beginning of his career, if by 'career' we understand a wild, uncontrolled downhill plummet to an unknown and perilous destination.

He returned the scroll and sat down to speak to the small group of people in front of him, and he said, 'Today this writing is fulfilled before you, even as I speak.'

This is how it all begins: no grandiose statement about his place in God's plan for his chosen people, no weighty verse about the Lord's warrior or the son of man, no sweet pastoral image of lambs and harvests: just these random verses, this obscure nonsense. Who was this convicted criminal, this stubborn son sentenced to shameful death? Not Jesus himself, certainly, for a more abstinent man could not have been imagined. No, in fact he could not even lay honest claim to that, for abstinence implies desire, and I knew my brother to be driven by the most fleshless soul that ever stalked the earth. I wondered if perhaps he so doubted the small store of humanity that he kept in his scrawny, pious chest that he wished he were capable of these little sins himself.

But my brother was no longer that brother I thought I knew: he was still speaking and I heard him say, 'Today these words can be erased from the scroll, for they have done their job. Do you want to know the way to life? I am the way. Yes, and the truth, and life itself, and this scripture is fulfilled in me. These words have no more flavour in them, for I am the one of whom they spoke, and what need can you have of dead scrolls when you have the living flesh of God before your eyes? Do you have the courage to take up the Law against God's own son? God desires to forgive, but he cannot forgive those who fail to sin. Which of you will do God's work with me?'

I was not comfortable to raise my voice in that sort of place, so I kept quiet, but the leaders of the synagogue began to mutter among themselves and say, 'How is it that he speaks to us like this? Surely he is possessed by an evil spirit who fills his mouth with nonsense and profane rubbish.'

Then Jesus spoke directly to them and said, 'If what I say is from the evil one, then where do you find the words you speak? But if I say what the Spirit has given me to say, then be sure that the word of God is among you. I tell you truly, at the end of days, when all your thoughts and deeds are sifted by the fire, all your foolishness will be forgiven but this, for anyone who blasphemes against the Spirit will not be pardoned, and whoever calls the holy Spirit evil is guilty of the only sin.'

I was mortified, but secretly proud to hear my brother speaking so powerfully in that place of hollowness and certainty, but the mood of the crowd was getting nasty, and my brothers and I stepped forward to take him home with us. Perhaps we should rather have attempted to stuff the south wind into a wineskin, for he scorned us and said, 'Who are you to call yourselves my family? I have the Spirit for my father, and from this day on I will choose my mother and my brothers and my sisters for myself', and he continued to preach.

Blessed are the lazy,
>   For they shall have rest.
Blessed are those who beg,
>   For to them will be given
>   And nothing asked in return.
Blessed are those who choose poverty,
>   For they shall fear no thief.
Blessed are those who have faith in themselves,
>   For their faith will be justified.
Blessed are those who honour their desires,
>   For their desires shall be without end.
Blessed are those who share all things,
>   For all things will be theirs to share.
Blessed are those who burn for justice,
>   For many will be guided by their light.
Blessed are the troublemakers,
>   For they shall be called children of God.
Blessed are the pure in heart,
>   For they shall be greater than God.

Do not doubt that I have come to abolish the Law and the Prophets: I am here not to piece together their dropped and broken words, but to sift and burn and smash them, and scatter the dust to the winds. For I tell you, if your purity does not surpass that of the Law and overturn the word of God, you will never find your place in heaven.

You have been told 'you shall not kill', but I say that if a person is hungry in your city or dies outside the gates of your town, it is as if you yourself had held a sword at their throat.

And you have been told 'you shall not commit adultery', but I say to you that marriage is nothing and adultery is nothing, but any man who looks upon a woman as an object or a thing to possess forfeits his right to justice, and any man who rapes a woman or a child or another man shall swiftly be torn limb from limb.

You have heard it said that you should love your neighbour and hate your enemy, but I say do not be like God, who sends one people to slaughter another and steal their land, but rather love all living things as you love yourselves.

Do not turn to see who is watching when you are about to do good. Seek neither the attention of onlookers nor the arrogance of secrecy, but give when the gift is needed, and with true love and generosity, that you who give and you who receive may enter heaven together. I tell you truly: give what it delights you to give and seek no reward but the joy of being alive, for those who give in the hope of getting in return will die alone and not be mourned, and those who store up wealth for themselves will find that their food turns to ashes in their mouths.

You ask me 'What is heaven like?' It is like a tiny seed which grows into a tree large enough for all to sit in its shade, just as a solitary refusal cast in the public eye grows into a whole new world of possibility. And again, it is like yeast mixed in with three measures of flour so that it is leavened right through, just as one impossible demand infects a thousand reasonable people and gives them the strength to change the world.

Come with me all who are lazy and are heavy-laden, and I will give you rest. Ask, and it will be given to you; seek, and you will find; knock, and the door will be opened to you. But if it is not given, steal, and if the door is locked against you, kick it down. For do not each of you give with open heart to those in need? Take, then, with open heart, when you find yourselves in need.

Do not worry about what you will eat, or what you will wear, for these things work themselves out. And do not worry about the future, for there is no future: nothing to plan for, nothing to wait for, nothing to save for. Simply live each day in the pleasures of each day, for when there is no future, how can there be sin? No true desire causes harm to another, but every unfulfilled desire is a sword in the hand of a maniac. Simply do what you wish to do, and live, and harm nothing: there is no other way to life.

You who crave purity and demand devotion are the very ones who stew in debauchery. You build prisons with your laws and brothels with your religion: you fear life and prevent others from finding it. Yet I tell you that when your years are done and your days are counted up and weighed, every sin will be forgiven except blasphemy against the desire to live. Only those who fear life will suffer death.

When Jesus had said these things, many of the people were enraged, and they wanted to take him to the gates of the town to stone him, but they were unable to, because so many others gathered around him to follow him into life. I was one of them. It was quite possible that he was entirely mad, that his time in the wilderness had slipped the last few knots that kept his mind among us, that in the next town he would succeed in getting himself stoned, but in the meantime I would stay with him. Yes, it is true: the last thing he needed was followers, and if I sinned at all it was in this.

4. We wandered the land

My brother's fame spread and many were convinced that he was a prophet, and we made our way throughout the region of Galilee, gathering. To all those who wished to be his disciples, Jesus said, 'Foxes have holes and birds have nests, but we will have no place to rest our heads.' He warned them of persecution, saying, 'The time will come when anyone who kills you will call it a holy service to God', and of calamity, saying, 'I have come to bring not peace, but a sword', but in spite of this a small, dedicated, ragged, foolhardy, adventurous, last-ditch band followed him. Some would stay with us for a while, then drift away, back to their old lives. Others would come with strong expectations and become disillusioned, and there would be fights and rifts and angry partings of ways: bitter expulsions of those who failed to live up to their promise, who took a hard line, who lacked humour, who failed to live in the present. Some would be ardent supporters whenever we were near their town, but never venture far beyond its gates. One man begged to be allowed to bury his father first, but Jesus replied, 'Drive your cart and your plough through the bones of the dead: we must blaze a trial to a new life.'

It was as the prophet Amos wrote: 'Just as the shepherd rescues a shin bone or the scrap of an ear from the lion's mouth, so will the remnant of Israel be saved.' There is no doubt that my crazy, sainted brother changed people's lives completely: some of us he turned inside out.

There are writers who have attempted to compile lists of those who travelled with us that winter, but they cannot even agree with each other. All the lists begin with Simon the fisherman, who left his boats, his nets, his house, his old mother: everything. There is justice in this, since it would be hard to find a more blindly obedient follower than he, and blind obedience is surely the most profitable form of ignorance. His brother Andrew certainly joined us for a while, but mainly out of fear of the responsibilities his brother's departure would have dumped on his shoulders, and he didn't last. James and John, the so-called Sons of Thunder, were a couple of boys whose chief pleasure (when they were not trying to coax violent miracles out of my brother) was to throw stones on people's roofs. Matthew indeed left his tax collecting as if it were a corpse he had been shackled to, just as Thomas left his labouring and Thaddeus his uncle's sheep, but of them only Thomas was there at the end. The only Philip I can recall was a scribe whose house we stayed at in Capernaum. The second James and the second Simon (and even, in one version, a second Judas) are clearly there just to make up a neat dozen, but what old Bartholomew is doing in the list I cannot imagine. Perhaps he rates an honourable mention for having made the sandals whose straps the mad baptiser was unworthy to untie, but he certainly never stirred beyond Nazareth on our account.

But on each of these lists, the final name is mine: Judas. They call me Judas the traitor, but I was the truest of my brother's followers. Even now, at this dry end of my life, I have spoken not one false word about him. He was the tree of life, and I was the axe of the apostles.

We had practically nothing except what we were: the cheapest paradise is to have nothing to lose.

We spoke the words of serpents in the tongues of angels; we sang the hymns of famine and plague. We spewed out old oaths, forgotten curses, damaged visions and buried desires. The simplest pun was a prophecy, the most outrageous insult a sermon: any verse of any sacred book was in danger of our fulfilment. We dressed in rags and demons and danced at funerals; we sang dirges in the market place; we painted ourselves with skin diseases, gate crashed weddings and flirted with the guests. We proclaimed every day a Sabbath, and refused to work. We proclaimed freedom from the Law. We announced the death of God, then turned and spat in his face. We wandered the land empty-handed, taking no money with us, not even a change of clothes. Whatever village we strayed into, we sought out people who would feed and house us, and if we found no one we would shake the dust from our feet and move on. We ate with tax collectors and drank with prostitutes. We turned people's comfortable worlds upside down in our search for diversion. What we saw in the dark we told in the daylight; what we heard whispered we called from the rooftops. There was much to be seen in the dark.

We did what we had to do. We did what made sense at the time: a determined, fanatical, crazed abolition of the past, to make way for a future which we knew may not exist, whose existence we actively denied. John's disciples abstained from everything in the name of purity, and the multitudes called them possessed. In the name of desire, we indulged in whatever appealed to us, and they called us glutton, drunkard, spendthrift, slut. We didn't bring peace on earth: we set son against father and daughter against mother. No one who preferred mother or father to us was worthy of us. No one who preferred son or daughter to us was worthy of us. In the end no one was worthy of us: we learned to hate our friends for the sins of the world. People said we thought it was the end times: that we were living in the last days. We didn't care. We were living in the only days there were. Every generation thinks itself the last, and only cowards require such justification. In those three short months, I experienced the most total nihilism and the most abject hope. Some days I felt that it was for this moment that humanity had been created, but in the end only children can live one day at a time and fail to see what they are letting slip through their fingers. The sweetest, cheapest paradise: to have nothing to lose. And to lose even that? The most pathetic fall.

5. No better place to look

What is it possible to say about Mary that has not been many times said? Only, I suppose, that I loved her more than any man, living or dead. It is true that she was a whore, that she made her living from the sticky traffic of men's dreams, but I loved her, and she was beautiful.

I was not, despite the rumours, in the habit of visiting prostitutes: once, when I was a very young man, I had paid for pleasure with one of the women of Magdala, but I had succeeded for years in keeping away from that ambiguously satisfying path. There were times, however, when I felt close to bursting with desire, and occasionally I was forced to return. I only ever visited these women when there seemed to be no alternative, when I needed sex so much that I felt I could no longer do without it, and so it hardly mattered to me that these women were strangers, and frequently quite unappealing strangers at that. I was there for a purpose, they were there to serve a precise function, and a simple, satisfying, profitable arrangement was reached on that basis.

When I met Mary, however, the situation was different. I was not full of lust in need of being spent, but simply lonely. I wanted more than anything to be loved, and the love I wanted was the warmth, the comfort, the closeness, the skin contact that I believed I could find with a woman. Sex was certainly part of the handful of sensations I desired, but it was not a large part of it. I wanted comfort for my soul and my whole self, yet I could think of no way in which I could achieve any form of satisfaction except with the women who I had once paid simply to sate my body. I wanted to be held, safe, rocked back and forth: the very things I had sometimes paid these women to do to one organ I now wanted done to my whole body, my whole self, my soul.

I went to the house of the women, not sure that I was strong enough to offer my trembling body to their scornful, professional arms, but sure enough that they were my only hope of feeling not alone. I was wise enough to know that I was looking for spiritual comfort in the wrong place, but also that there was no better place to look. My brother had frequently claimed that God was love, but I had never understood what he meant. For me, women were always love: my mother Mary, my wife Mary, and all the women in between. God never held my hand or rocked me in his arms. He never whispered comfort in my ear, or smelled of cinnamon and bread. The sight of his naked back never put my heart at ease, and there was no place that I ever found within him where I could be safe from fear and safe from being alone. So perhaps Mary was my god. Perhaps that is why I kissed her feet and sang her praise.

She smiled at me. I hadn't expected a smile. Some of the whores had bared their teeth in my direction with the same utter lack of conviction with which they had flaunted their naked breasts, but this woman smiled as if she were happy to see me, as if I were already, in some sense, her friend, and I was quite prepared to let that make me feel good.

I asked her name, and she said, 'Mary.'

I was about to tell her mine when she put her finger to my lips and said, 'And I know who you are.'

I guessed that this could have only been from one of the other women in the house, and I felt flattered that I had been discussed. We smiled at each other: I'm sure we made a great couple. I felt very warm towards her. I felt that she was a lovely person. I felt glad to have met her, and entirely at ease in her company. This was exactly what I had barely hoped to find. As we climbed the stairs to the upper room, I put my arm around her. She seemed a little surprised, but settled into it as if the surprise were a matter of such familiarity being rare, but not unwelcome. I was amazed at how good it felt: if it was all an act, it was a very pleasant one. I was not, I assured myself, falling in love. Falling was far too accidental a word for this.

Then, when we got to the room and she started to get ready,

everything seemed to change, and I began to feel awkward. I wasn't sure that I wouldn't have preferred to give her my money just to spend the time talking and holding each other. Downstairs I had felt like we were friends: here it felt like it was all too quick and too unreal. She did what she did in a way that indicated long-established routine: I stood next to the couch feeling lost.

She saw my look and said, 'Why don't you get undressed?'

It wasn't a question, but if it had been I would have answered it like this: I was worried that having sex would spoil the friendship. It was hard to pretend that we were here for anything other than business, and that was exactly what I needed to be able to pretend. I wanted to be loved, and I was prepared to pay for the illusion of being loved, but I wasn't so easily fooled. Somewhere in my head was a little voice saying, 'You don't know this woman, and she doesn't love you', and it overrode all the feelings and all the physical sensations.

She massaged my half-erect organ, without succeeding in exciting it to greater rigidity. She stroked it and fondled my balls; I caressed her breasts, which were magnificent, and her buttocks, and her waist and hips and shoulders, none of which were in any way less than exactly what I would have desired, had desire been my motive. In my heart: distress; from my loins, no response.

She began to get concerned: I guess it went to the heart of her professional skills. She worried that I was cold, but that wasn't the problem. She asked, 'What's wrong? Don't you find me attractive?' and I reassured her that I did – that I could not, in fact, have found her more beautiful – but that it just didn't feel like the real thing.

She seemed amused: 'Of course it's not the real thing: that's why you're paying for it. Most men don't want it to be the real thing. That's what they come here for: something different.'

I didn't want to hear that. I didn't want to know about most men, or the fact that there were other men, had been other men, would be other men. I wanted the real thing. For me the real thing would have been something different. I wanted her to love me.

She kept asking and asking, 'What can I do? What would you like me to do? Is there anything I can do?' and I kept lying and lying 'I don't know, I don't know, I don't know', when I was perfectly well aware that what I wanted, what I needed, what would work, was utterly forbidden: I wanted her to kiss me.

I ended up on my back, with Mary lying on top of me. In its own way, this was very pleasant; it made it easy to cup her gorgeous buttocks, to hold her waist, to stroke her thick, black hair. I kept running my fingers through her hair, over the back of her scalp, wanting to pull her head down towards my face, knowing that it was exactly what I would not be allowed to do.

There was a knock on the door, and I expected Mary to tell me that my time was up, but she just called out 'Okay' and said to me 'Don't worry about that.' She asked me again, 'Is there anything I can do that will help?' and I, feeling that there was little left to lose, said, 'I know that it's not what you do, but I really wish you would kiss me.'

She said, 'No, I don't do that', but then she leaned down towards me so her face was close to mine. Her hair fell on my cheeks, and I could feel her breath on my face, and after a moment's pause she brushed her lips against mine. It was the slightest touch – the barest mime of kissing – but it worked: partly for the pure sensation, and partly because I knew it was such a special favour. The response was immediate, and she was able to take hold of me and squeeze me inside her. It felt wonderful, and she looked happy and relieved, and we began to move, and it was lovely.

It didn't take me long, having been so tense, and as I came she rested her face against my cheek, and I held her just as if it was the real thing, and I almost cried. I kissed her on the forehead, and she didn't pull away.

As we were getting dressed, both flushed with exertion and pleasure, she said, 'I enjoyed that. It felt good', and I, not wanting to be a fool, said, 'I'm not sure that I can believe you.'

She seemed a little hurt, and said. 'You can believe what you like, but I'm telling you: most times I don't feel anything much, but sometimes it sort of sneaks up on you, and this was one of those times.'

Perhaps it was because of the talking, and the fact that I had taken so long to get started, stroking her and kissing her breasts, but it felt nice to be told that I had given her pleasure too. She was a real delight. I think it was at that moment, if it happens in a single moment, that I fell in love with her.

We went down the stairs together, and when we reached the door I turned to say goodnight, but when I saw her face I stopped. Her eyes were deep and dark and glowed like comets, and as I looked at her she touched my wrist. Her lips were so soft and beautiful: her whole mouth asked to be kissed, and I obeyed. It was cold enough to see our breath, but we held each other in the doorway of that house of flesh, and we kissed. We kissed like innocents, like a mother suckling her child, like lovers who don't know when they will ever kiss again. We kissed each other as if kissing were breathing, and then I went out, and it was night.

6. Not a blade of grass withers

Some few days later – days spent thinking of nothing but my Mary – we were in Capernaum, on our way to the house of a relatively minor local bureaucrat named Jairus, whose daughter was close to death.

Jesus loved these moments when he could turn someone's private tragedy into an opportunity for gathering a crowd and being profound. To those who he healed, his words were always 'Your faith has made you well', but we all knew clearly enough that he could have made them well whether they had faith or not. When it pleased him, he could cast a cloud of demons out of a raving Gadarene and send them screaming into a herd of swine; in a different moment and a darker mood he would tell a Syrian woman that to waste a miracle on a gentile would be to throw the children's bread to the dogs, and this when he had just finished feeding a multitude with a couple of loaves. If he chose, he could heal a Roman soldier's servant at a distance of eight miles, simply by speaking a word, but on this occasion, knowing that the sick girl had her hand on the gate of death, and seeing the anguish in her father's face, he felt the need to visit her in person.

As we were walking along the road, trailing a swarm of followers, I saw Mary. She was pushing her way through the crowd, trying to get close to us, and with a lover's keen sense of his beloved's presence I could smell her: the same beautiful hot stink of carnal activity that I had smelt on my hands and on my body the day after I had met her, when I had been so happy that I could barely believe that I was alive.

I smelt her, and I saw her, but she was looking past me: she was right behind Jesus, and it was him that she was pressing towards, not me. She reached him, she touched his robe, and he stopped.

He turned and looked at this stranger, my wife, and said, 'Who touched me?'

Jairus could not believe that he would interrupt this farcical procession to ask such a foolish question, when we were being jostled all around by the masses, and tried to upbraid him for his thoughtlessness, but Jesus's glare and the man's awareness of his own need shut his mouth.

I too tried to speak, but what I said, no one remembers, because Jesus spoke again and said, 'I felt someone touch me, and I lost something of myself in that touch. Who was it?'

Mary, who had looked radiant some moments before, dropped her gaze from his face, and he asked her directly, 'Woman, who are you?'

She answered, 'For five days since we met I have thought of nothing else but our meeting, and I have been wet the whole time thinking of you, but when I touched your robe and you spoke to me like that, I dried up. Is this how you treat those you love? Is this the love of God?'

Jesus replied, 'Shameless woman. Who told you that I loved you? Who are you that I should stop here and love you, when I have such important work to do?'

The little girl's anxious father was almost tearing his fingers off with wringing his hands throughout this, and the pitiful smile he directed at my brother was the reflex of a cornered and desperate man.

Mary tried to meet my brother's eyes, but they were as hard and sharp as spears, and she did not have the strength. She was barely audible as she asked, 'Do you not know me, my Lord? Do you remember nothing?' and Jesus answered from the full height of his self assurance, saying, 'Woman, I remember everything. Not a blade of grass withers, not a sparrow falls from the sky without my knowing it, but you I do not know.'

She replied, with a confidence built on the quick flame of anger, 'But you knew me, my Lord. You knew me. You came to me lonely, and I gave you strength. You were hungry and I fed you, thirsty and I suckled you. You were small and cold and trembling, and I warmed you between my thighs and held you tight inside me until you shook. You came to me in pieces and I made you whole. You came to me in the dark of night and left with the stars in your eyes. You came to me alone and I gave myself to you, and you need never have been alone again, but you have taken these gifts and thrown them in the dust like stale bread. For this blasphemy you will die. You will not live long enough to understand what men and women mean when we talk of love.'

Jesus was stopped by this confusing outburst, and raised his hands to cast out the demons within her, saying, 'Spirit of grief, spirit of destruction, loosen your hold and come out of her now', but nothing happened, because there was nothing evil within her.

Jairus touched my brother's sleeve to remind him of a prior – and urgent – engagement, but Jesus snapped at him and said, 'Be quiet, man. Your boy will live without requiring a single word from you.'

But before the man could correct the misapprehension about his daughter's gender, his servant arrived and told him, 'Master, there is no need to trouble the teacher any more. She has died.'

Jairus fell on his knees in the dust and began to weep, and the crowd began to mutter against Jesus and against Mary, but he told them, 'You are fools who have not the faith to open your eyes in the morning and believe that there is light. Those who wish to see the power of God will see that all things are possible for me. And you, woman,' he said to Mary, 'must confess your lies and follow humbly in my steps if you wish to be saved.'

I had been silent all this time, but I was by then standing next to Mary, and I put my hand on her arm and said, 'Brother, be calm. Mary is not lying, but simply mistaken. It was I, not you, who benefited from her generosity: I who witnessed the miracles of skin and warmth, and was blessed with her love and kisses. Mary,' I addressed her, 'it was me you loved, and to me you gave yourself, and I accept that gift. My brother knows nothing of you, but you know everything of me.'

Mary looked at me with an expression at first puzzled, but then disappointed, as she realised that I was speaking the truth. 'What is your name?' she asked, and I replied, 'Judas.'

'Judas', she repeated, weighing the word as if a choice were to be made on the basis of its sound. 'You are his brother?'

I nodded in answer, and she asked, 'So are you also the son of God?'

'No,' I admitted, 'my father was a carpenter.'

'Then I have been mistaken. Perhaps your name should be Jacob, for you have come by stealth and stolen your brother's blessing.'

There are things you don't say: things you leave unsaid. There are things that it does not help to say out loud. I replied as lightly as my heart would permit, trying to use a touch of humour, trying to sound like a man in love, trying not to beg: 'And I have been mistaken too, if your gifts were intended for another man, for I came without guile and without disguise. You gave me life, and I have not forgotten a moment of the time we spent together, or the love you showed me. Can you give life and then take it back so soon? Am I not, in fact, the man you loved so well, so fully, so miraculously?'

There are things you don't say. There are fists you don't form, blows you don't make, punches you don't aim, stones you don't throw. There are teeth you don't bare, eyes you don't gouge, bones you leave unshattered, skulls you leave intact. But when you aim your bitterness at someone's heart – an easy, innocent heart, a heart full of love – you forget all that, and you speak like this: 'So it would seem, and yet you are not the man I love. I cannot say how or why I love your brother, but the truth is that I do. Had I not loved your brother first, perhaps I would love you, but to he who has, more shall be given, while from he who has not, even what he has will be taken away.'

Now is the time to curse me, if you believe that I am a traitor, if you believe that I, of all the people in the world, have sinned in this. Condemn me, all of you who understand what it was to drag my body along that road – and other dusty roads and other days – watching my loveless brother play god and my Mary try without success to be his wife. Pick up those stones, you judges: those wide, flat, round stones that bring such peace of mind to the pious. Bury me, broken, beneath them, but tell me first what else I should have done. Explain to me how I was meant to care that Jairus's little girl was summoned back to life the moment my brother told her to get up. Explain to me how anything other than pain was possible: to have found paradise, and to be held back from its gate by those who did not wish to enter.

7. If your eye causes you to sin

Two weeks later it was Purim, we were still in Capernaum, and we were drunk. It is the one day of the year when drunkenness and irresponsible noise are sanctioned by our religion, as we celebrate the day Queen Esther saved the people from the hands of the evil Haman, may his name be erased from memory. On this day, of all the days of the year, I felt most at home with my culture, and it was unable to censure my behaviour.

We were having a great time, being drunk and loud and Jewish all at once, when Jesus stood up and called to us to follow him.

As we were walking – stumbling behind him as he led us up a nearby hill – he asked us, 'Do you know who I am? Who am I?' and we all answered, with more or less clarity of conviction, that he was Jesus, but he asked us again, 'What are they saying about me?'

Since this was one of the increasingly rare moments when there was not some sort of crowd nearby, it was not immediately clear to our foggy minds exactly what he meant.

Mary, always close to him, asked, 'Who are you talking about? Who is talking about you?' and Jesus said, 'The crowds. The people. What do they say about me? Who do they say I am?'

Matthew and Thaddeus started repeating all the things we had heard people saying: that my brother was either Elijah, or another of the prophets, or John the Baptist returned to life, or indeed utterly mad.

'But what about you?' he asked, 'who do you say that I am?'

Well, I knew who he was. I had grown up with him, shared a bath and a bed with him, watched him develop from a painfully vague boy into this curious mixture of arrogance and saintliness who asked these absurd questions. Who did I say he was? He was Jesus, my older brother, the one who claimed that almighty God had impregnated his mother – my mother – and that he was the result. The one who claimed to be the only son of God, to have rejected all temptation, to have been sent to save the world. He was my wife's husband, but he was not me: he was the thorn in my side, the pebble between my toes, the dust in my eye.

Then simple-minded Simon, bless his soul, piped up and said, 'Surely you are the Messiah', and Jesus turned on him furiously, screaming like an entirely crazy man, and saying, 'Get out of my way, you fool. You used to be called Simon, but I will call you Peter, because you are a rock placed in my path. You are a stumbling block, a foolishness, a lump. Don't you realise that the Messiah is destined to be rejected, to suffer grievously and be put to death? Are you so unfamiliar with the scriptures? Just as Moses lifted up the serpent in the wilderness, so the son of man is to be lifted up on a cross for the redemption of the people. What is there to gain by winning the whole world and losing my life? And what can I give in exchange for my life? Am I to suffer for the likes of you?'

He told us then never to tell anyone that he was the Messiah: I had never seen him recoil from his destiny like that. And suddenly the light shone upon him, and it looked as if he was glowing white, right there in the middle of us, transfigured. His clothes were brilliant, and his face was dazzling, and he was overcome with fear and began to cry like a child: he didn't know what to say, he was so frightened.

Then a cloud seemed to swallow us all up, and I imagined God up there saying, 'This is my son? My chosen one? My beloved? Listen to him. If he is ashamed of me, then I will be ashamed of him. Anyone who wants to save his life will lose it, but anyone who loses his life for my sake will save it. Once the hand is on the plough, no one who turns back is fit for the kingdom of God.'

Then the cloud vanished and the sky was dark, and he begged us not to talk about what we had seen – not to say a word about it – and

I wondered how this coward brother of mine could dare to show his face in the company of the prophets. Simon was still smarting from having been told off before, so he wasn't going to say anything, and Thaddeus and Thomas were muttering to each other about signs from heaven. None of them seemed to think that there was anything wrong with being told to keep all this a secret, and none of them said a word when my scared and suffering brother consented to rest his head on Mary's breasts, and she led him off to share with him the comfort which nature had uniquely equipped her to give.

In this, my brother was quite unlike John the Baptist, who had such an aversion to fleshly pleasures – both in others and in himself – that he had eventually been imprisoned for telling King Herod that he should not marry Herodias, his brother Philip's wife. It seems that Herod was afraid of John's effect on his public standing, but privately had a great deal of time for him, and treated him with a mixture of respect and fear. Herodias, on the other hand, resented being called a whore in public, and wanted John dead. The story that is told of this is that, while John was locked up in Herod's palace, he came to the attention of Herodias' daughter Salome. She was a young girl, barely old enough to marry, but she had such a strong desire for John that she could not leave him alone. She would visit him in the room where he was imprisoned and attempt to seduce him, supplementing her natural charms with all the art she could command, with offers of freedom, and with threats of execution. She would kiss his manacled hands, she would twine her fragrant arms around his unwashed chest, she would bribe his guards to lock her in his cell overnight, wearing nothing but a veil, but nothing could persuade the mad, grizzled, dangerously saintly Baptist to mingle his rough and hairy body with this smooth and passionate girl, and so she formed an insatiable desire to possess him by other means.

One evening, as Herod was celebrating his birthday with a banquet for the wealthy and powerful people of his circle, Salome entered the banqueting hall and danced before the king and his guests, and into this dance she poured all the passion and all the frustration of her months of failed seduction. The nobles were entranced by this young virgin who danced so expertly, and Herod – having taken his brother's wife, and clearly not indifferent to her daughter – was so moved that he called her to him and swore an oath before all the people there, saying, 'For this dance, I will give you anything you ask, even up to half my kingdom.'

Salome swiftly replied, 'I want the head of John the Baptist brought to me on a platter.'

Herod was shocked by her request, but did not wish to deny her for fear that she would deny the approach he wished to make later that evening, but still he could not bring himself to execute his prisoner, so he replied to her, 'My daughter, what you ask is more than I can give: I said I would give you up to half my kingdom, but what you have requested is greater than that. I cannot shed the blood of this righteous man.'

That night Salome took a knife and went to the Baptist's cell, and when he slept she drove the blade through his throat and hacked his head from his shoulders. That same night Herod left his bed and went to Salome's empty chamber, and her servant led him to where she sat at the dead man's feet, holding his head in her lap, running her fingers through its hair and kissing its bloodied lips.

So on that night – that single night – that Jesus spent in Mary's arms, I lay awake, turning this story over in my mind, setting him up against John's stern, unnatural resolution, nurturing the secret love that would make my brother immortal. It is a shameful thing for a private erotic struggle to be played out in the public eye, and an insane irony for its tragic climax to become the cornerstone of a religion, but I was not the one who set the conditions. After all, can the wedding party mourn when the bridegroom is among them? First we must get rid of the groom, and then the mourning can begin. My brother should have known. Had he listened to his own words, he would have known the truth. He could have had all the women he desired – although in fact he desired none – for there was no shortage of followers wishing to be filled with the love of God. Instead he chose the woman who owned my heart. She was my own flesh and life: what God had joined together he should not have divided. Well, if your eye causes you to sin, pluck it out, and if your brother sins against you, cut him off, for is it not better to enter into paradise without your brother, than to keep him and be condemned in hell?

The following morning I confronted Jesus and said to him, 'Moses and Elijah suffered for our people. They were called by their god, they stood up for what they believed, and they were prepared to suffer for it. You claim divinity, which neither of them did, yet you are too afraid to let it even be talked about. Are you ashamed of your god? Are you capable of doing what he chose you to do? If you are who you claim to be, then have the courage to stand in the temple and tell the world. No Messiah should lead this easy Galilean life, teaching in small-town synagogues and preaching to the fisherman and the shepherds. If the world is to be won, then Jerusalem is the place to be.'

My brother looked me in the eye, weighed up my words, released himself from Mary's hands, stood up straight and said, 'Thank you, my brother, for showing me my error. The tempter led me from the path, but you have shown me where to place my feet. You are the truest of my apostles, for you cannot bear to see me be less than myself. Thank you, Judas.'

Then, turning from me to the others, he announced, 'My friends, we must leave this place: my business here is over. There are things that must be done, and the whole world groans until they are brought to completion. The son of man must stand before his people and proclaim the kingdom of God, without fear of what will follow. In Jerusalem, where the vultures are: that is where the corpses gather.'

This wasn't exactly what I had expected. I had hoped to humiliate him: take him at a moment of vulnerability, present him with a stark and dangerous choice, and watch him fail. I wanted Mary to see the mismatch between his rhetoric and his courage, but – being an unbeliever – I had forgotten about faith. I had simply failed to realise that his sense of mission was strong enough to overcome his fear. I had hoped to ruin him, and now I had to walk with him those dusty roads to death. The night before, Jesus had been a normal, sensual man, but now, when he fell on his knees and begged his god to forgive his weakness, we knew that it was not simply his moment of fear that troubled him, but his acceptance of love. He was no longer Mary's husband now: he was wedded to his destiny – even to his death – and he would keep her at a distance. He still loved her and walked beside her, but he would not let her hold him or caress him or kiss him, as she expected to do.

Mary did not try to overcome her desires: she was weeping and furious and unbelieving; she teased him and flirted with him and tried to tempt him, but he gritted his teeth and turned from her. I found this even harder to witness than the brief intimacy of the night before. It had been painful enough to watch the woman I adored adoring my brother, but now I was forced to endure the spectacle of this most beautiful and desirable of women throwing herself in the way of a man who resolutely closed his eyes to her. If I could have torn my eyes away I would not have seen her bare her breasts to him and be rejected. If I could have torn my feet away I would not have followed them and multiplied my grief. If I had had a choice I could have chosen, but I could never return to my workshop to make beds which Mary and I would never sleep in, tables we would never eat at, doors through which I would never carry her as my bride. Our pain – this I learned – is ours alone, and we must not fail it when it needs us.

8. Behold: a man had two sons

To get to Jerusalem, where dead prophets are honoured, we had to pass through Samaria, as we had done many times before: dusty pilgrims on a dangerous road. On the first day we came to a village in the heat of the afternoon and found a well, and there was a woman there, drawing water. In these villages, virtuous women gather in the evening to draw water and to gossip and to exchange the stories of the day, and it was clear enough that this woman would feature heavily in the stories of those good Samaritan wives: her face was unveiled, and she didn't rush to cover it when she saw a group of strangers approaching. Nor, indeed, did she turn her head away when a strange man – my brother – addressed her and asked her for water.

No doubt Mary recognised her as a fellow merchant in dreams and flesh, and no doubt Jesus recognised, if nothing else, that recognition.

He asked her for water, and she flashed her eyes at him and replied, 'Why is it that a teacher like yourself asks to drink from a woman like me? Can none of your followers cool your thirst?'

Jesus, stung by this attack on his freshly minted chastity, spoke back to her, saying, 'If you knew who it is that you were talking to, you would ask me for the water I can give you.'

The woman's face broke into a smile, and she asked, 'God's gift to women, are you?' then she turned to Mary and asked her, 'Is it true, my sister? From the look in your eye, I would say there is no one better placed to judge.'

'Indeed he is God's gift,' my darling replied, 'but not in the way that you suppose he means. If you were to ask him the right question he would give you the water of life, which would mean that you would never thirst again.'

'That would be a gift even worth begging a man for,' said the woman, and she asked Jesus, 'So what is the right question to ask so that you will give me this living water?'

To which he replied, 'Go and bring your husband here.'

'I don't have a husband,' scoffed the woman, and Jesus replied, 'Of course not. You have had five husbands, Martha, and the man you had last night was not one of them.'

'I see you are a prophet,' said the woman. 'Martha is indeed my name, and the man I took in last night is not the kind that I would sleep with for nothing. So tell me, prophet: where should we worship God? On our Mount Gerazim, or in Jerusalem?'

Jesus answered her, putting his hand on her shoulder, 'When you are in Samaria, you worship God in Samaria, and when you are in Jerusalem you worship there. This mountain or another is all the same, my friend. Worship God truly, with your soul and with your body, and it makes no difference where you are.'

Hearing this, Martha of Sychar said, 'Teacher, I would be pleased if you and your friends would share a meal with me and lodge with me tonight', and she took her water jar and led us back to the village.

As we went into the house of the prostitute, she let it be known that she would not receive any clients that night. Once inside, she set about preparing a meal for us all, and she complained to Jesus that Mary did not offer to help, but simply sat at the feet of the man she loved, listening to his words and gazing at his face.

Jesus told her, 'What Mary has chosen is the better way. I will be here only for a short time, and she has chosen to hear my words.'

Martha was not impressed, since she had little choice but to feed her guests, and I went into the kitchen to help her. She scoffed at the idea of a man offering to help to prepare a meal, and I readily admitted that it was not the ideal workshop for my skills, but I explained to her that I loved the company of women, and I could not bear to sit and watch the woman I adored fawning for my brother's attention. This tough-hearted woman of many men saw the love and the pain in my eyes and the frustration in my heart, and she let me help her prepare the meal, although it is quite possible that I actually slowed the process down. And after we had eaten and cleared the things away, I slept with her in her soft bed, while the others slept on mats in the main room. We didn't know each other, as the saying goes – that was not part of the deal – but she slept beside me, soft and warm and female, and she filled the hunger of my body with that best of things: a woman's skin. She slept in my arms, my one hand on her belly and the other on her breasts, and I nestled hard between her buttocks. My body longed to push inside her, but I knew that I could not betray my wife like that, so I lay there, awake, listening to the breathing of this kind stranger, and breathing in the scent of her hair.

In the morning, a crowd gathered outside to hear the words of the prophet who had brought his followers to stay in the house of a prostitute, and he spoke to them in riddles, because really he was speaking to me, rebuking me for the sin he could not believe I had not committed.

He said, 'Behold: a man had two sons, and one day he said to them, "My sons, today you must work in the vineyard." Now the first son said, "I will not", but later changed his mind and went, while the second said, "Certainly", but did not go. Which of these sons did his father's bidding?'

I was in no mood to be publicly chided by someone so newly holy as my brother, so I replied to him, 'No doubt you will tell me that the elder son did his father's bidding, but I would say that at the end of the day both will be punished, because one failed to work, and the other failed to submit. Do you think the kingdom of heaven has places set for liars? Surely you are mistaken.'

Then I continued with another story: 'Another man had two sons who he sent to work in another man's field. The eldest son went to work at daybreak for a good day's wage and toiled all day in the sun, while his brother was not to be found. Then as the day's work was nearly done, the landowner saw the second son in the marketplace and said to him, "Get to work in my field also, and I will pay you what is fair", so the second son also went to work. At the end of the day, when the landowner paid his workers, those he had hired last he paid first, giving them a full day's wage. When the first hired came to be paid they expected more, having worked all day, but he gave them the same amount: just what they had agreed. When they grumbled against him he answered their complaint, saying to the first son, "I gave to your brother what I wished to give. Is it a fault that I am too generous? But as for your greediness, you may be sure that your father will hear of this." What do you say to that, my virtuous teacher? In the kingdom of heaven, the last shall be first, and the first shall be last.'

Jesus was angry that I had spoken against him in front of these Samaritans, and he challenged me with another story. 'A third man planted a vineyard, leased it to tenants, and went abroad. When the harvest time came, he sent a servant to collect his share of the crop, but the tenants beat him and sent him home empty handed. The owner sent another servant, and another, but they too were beaten and sent away. Then the owner sent his two beloved sons, thinking, "They will respect my sons", but the younger son said to the tenants, "Beat my brother also, and kill him, for then the inheritance will be mine, and I will share it with you." When they had done this, he tore his clothes and went home in mourning, and what will his father do? Of course he will go and put those tenants to the sword, and his son will share the inheritance with no one.'

How was I to answer a charge like that? Was I my brother's murderer? What inheritance did we have to divide, apart from the workshop we had both abandoned for this life on the road? Did he think I would kill him for Mary's love? I was blind with aggrieved rage at this most unjust accusation, but before I could find words to reply, Mary herself spoke up, trying to show up our foolishness, and thus end our quarrel.

'A fourth man also had two sons, and the younger one said to him, "Father, divide the property between us, and give me my share now", and the man did as his son had asked. A few days later, the young man sold his share of the property and set off for the city, where he squandered his money on wine and fickle friends. After his wealth was all gone, he realised he would soon have to look for work or he would starve, but he thought to himself, "My father has hired men who have all they need, and here am I faced with hunger. I will go back to my father's house and throw myself on his mercy and beat my breast and beg to be his servant, and he will make me his son again in spite of all that I have done." So he left the city and went back to his father's house. While he was still some way off, he saw his father sitting in the dust before the gate, so he rushed to him and said, "Father, I am a fool and a sinner, and no longer deserve to be called your son. Take me back as one of your hired men, so that I may repay your goodness to me." The father looked bitterly at his son and replied, "You are more of a fool than you think. Since you left the house and wasted your inheritance, your brother has done just the same as you have done, and all our wealth is gone. You can work and you can beg, but you can never repay what you have taken from me." And so the son fell face down in the dust, and wept over his foolishness.'

Jesus and I exchanged remorseful glances, but neither of us was prepared to accept the responsibility for this public outburst. We could both see the sense in Mary's argument: we were both fools, fussing over what we couldn't change, robbing ourselves of the thing we both loved. But I resented the way Mary loved him, and the way he was prepared to spurn such a gift, and he despised me for being so much a slave to my skin that I would sleep in a stranger's arms, in the same house as the woman I loved. I hid from myself the effort it cost Jesus to keep his body pure, partly because I felt it was work wasted, but more because I could despise him better if I could pretend that he could overcome his desires only because his desires were so weak. Martha saw through us all – through my hypocrisy, through Jesus's strained excess of zeal, and through Mary's fear of conflict – and her story answered our shrill, self-serving pieties with a rich, fleshy mass of ancestral obscenity that I no longer see the need to repeat: a burst of creation pornography that sent the pious running to cover their ears, and the vulgar into gales of mirth.

The people of Sychar may not have been prepared to have Martha speak for them on many matters, but they were more than prepared to bask in her hard-earned wisdom on the topic of sexual rivalry, and Jesus wisely chose not to attempt to preach that day. This woman who had wrapped me in her gentle skin to sleep now flayed me in the village square. She left no doubt that these people who had arrived as a band of travellers peddling faith would be remembered as a pair of brothers fighting over a whore.

9. The salvation of our people

As we approached Jerusalem, we came to the place where my parents had once realised – twenty years earlier – that Jesus was no longer with us. He had no idea that this place had any special significance for me.

Once before, my dreams had been broken here: I would not be the eldest son after all. This time, I felt that the dream would be repaired – that soon I would be my mother's eldest son – but that was not my dream any more. I looked at him again, my crazy brother, and saw that he was again no longer with us. When I was a boy I saw him stay behind in Jerusalem, the city of God, of the temple, of the crowds, and at this place I was told that we must go back and drag him with us into a life of mere mortality. This time, as a man, I looked at his face and saw that he was in Jerusalem already, and this time no parents would drag him from his chosen path: mere mortality could not hold him. It was as if his fate were written on his forehead, or hung around his neck, or nailed to his wrists.

He sent one of the men who was with us to find a donkey so he could ride it into the city, but many who were there remembered the words of the prophet Zechariah and saw in this not an image of humility, but the start of a holy war.

When we reached the Mount of Olives, many of the followers began to sing his praises in words like these:

Punishment has come,
Retribution is here:
Blessed is he who comes in the name of the Lord;
Blessed is the son of David.
What is the sin of Judah?
Is it not Jerusalem?

This city hates those who teach justice at its gates
    And detests those who speak the truth.
You have ploughed malice and reaped treachery
    And the fruit of your harvest is deceit,
But against an idea – even a false one –
    All weapons are powerless.

In those days it seemed that you couldn't buy a loaf of bread without hearing the baker's theories about the coming of the Messiah. Every street vendor, merchant, beggar and whore had their ideas about the one who was to be the salvation of our people, and all the thoughts of all these people – the grandiose, the pious, the violent, the serene – whirled like clouds around my brother's other-worldly head.

When we entered Jerusalem, it seemed that the whole city was in turmoil as people asked, 'Who is this man? What has he come to do? What do the scriptures say about him?' and others answered, 'It is Jesus, the prophet, the one who was promised to us, the one who will bring us the victory.'

His opponents – the men whose job it was to keep the temporal rule of the Romans as far as possible from the business of religion – began to plot ways to remove him from the public eye and thus keep the peace.

Since so many of the followers were expecting a warrior king, some of the priests proposed a test, so they came to us in the midst of the crowds and asked him, 'Tell us, teacher, is it lawful to pay taxes to the Romans, or is it an act of disloyalty?'

Jesus said to them, 'Show me the coins you use to pay the taxes', and they showed him a Roman coin.

He asked, 'Whose head is this on the coin, and whose name?' and the priests said, 'Caesar's', so Jesus replied, 'Then give it to him if he asks for it, but be sure to give God what is his.'

They should have asked him did he therefore believe that there were things which were not God's, but they dodged the other way and asked, 'So you agree that the Romans are our legitimate rulers, do you?'

and Jesus sidestepped them by saying, 'The kingdom of God is not to be won with swords, but is a thing of the heart.'

His questioners realised they had let him escape to the high ground of mysticism, where the arrows of logic cannot penetrate, so they left us and returned to their plotting.

We were close to the temple, and many of the followers were in awe of the building and its opulence, but Jesus said to them, 'These stones? They impress you? This will not last. Woe to you who sleep now, for you shall be woken by the sound of rioting and Jerusalem will burn with the heat of many dreams. Not one of these stones will be left to rest against another: they will be crushed and scattered like the seeds from a handful of olives. And from these ruins I will build a new temple, not of stones, but of human hearts. My temple will be mightier than this, but it will not shine with splendour and make the visitor tremble. No, my temple will be seen only by those who dwell within it, and it will be the house of the living God, and it will last through the ages. No army will burn it, and no siege destroy it. No invader will carry off its treasures, and no king will set his name above the door. There will be no priests but the hearts which make up its walls, and no sacrifices but the love within those hearts. You don't set fire to a city only to hide it under a basket. No, when you light up a city, you must place it high on a sacred hill so that many may see its light. Oh, Jerusalem, how often have I desired to burn you in all your arrogant pride, just as your God destroyed the cities of the plain. Who then could tell the difference between Zion and Gehenna? And who would care? When the temple is destroyed, surely then the God is dead? Surely the God who commanded the destruction of Jericho will fall when his words turn back against his own holy city. Believe that it will be done to Jerusalem as it was in the days of Joshua: then my dreams will be fulfilled and dashed to pieces, for what I have proclaimed will come to pass. Burn well, fair city. Burn well, brave soldiers. Burn well, loyal citizens.'

When we went with Jesus into that same temple and saw the

traders selling doves and cattle to be sacrificed, and saw the money changers with their tables, offering kosher currency at exorbitant rates of exchange, he asked them, 'Is this a house of prayer, or is it a marketplace?'

One wealthy young man called John approached him and asked, 'Good teacher, what must I do to inherit eternal life?'

Jesus looked straight through him and said, 'You know the commandments: keep them.'

John looked shocked and replied, 'The commandments? I have always kept those. I do not steal, I do not kill, I do not commit adultery, I observe the sabbath', but Jesus returned, 'Then one more thing is needed: sell everything you own and give the money to the poor. Then you will have treasure in heaven.'

He then pointed to the temple treasury box, where people were putting their offerings. Some rich people were putting in quite generous amounts, but amongst them was a poor widow who put in two small coins, the smallest of coins, which lie in the dust of the road until someone is desperate enough to stoop and pick them up.

Jesus turned to the confused young man and said, 'Truly this poor widow has put in more than any of these rich people, for in their wealth they gave what they could spare, but in her poverty she put in all she had to live on. How hard it is for the rich to enter the kingdom of Heaven. I tell you it is easier for a camel to pass through the eye of a needle than for a rich person to enter the kingdom.'

'Certainly she is generous,' the young man continued, 'but surely she is not wise. What will she do now? She will have to beg or steal in order to live, for the priests have taken everything that was hers, just as they have stolen her every moral impulse and sold them back to her as ritual and piety. How will she live?'

Jesus looked deeply into his eyes and said, 'Young man, you asked me how to enter heaven, and now you are concerned with how to live on earth. Which one do you want? This woman has her eyes on heaven, and she will be there sooner than you.'

'Then it is not possible to have life on earth and then in heaven?' asked John.

'No,' said Jesus, 'It is not.'

When the traders heard what Jesus was saying they mocked him. Then, making a whip out of cords, he chased them from the temple courtyards, overturning the tables of the moneychangers and scattering those who were selling livestock. The priests and legal specialists were furious at my brother's destructive outburst, and they cornered him and demanded that he tell them where he got the authority to act so outrageously.

As he often did, he turned the question back on them, and asked, 'Tell me first: did John's baptism come from God, or was it all his own idea?'

His opponents were unable to answer him: they were not about to say that the scrawny mad man in the desert was the spokesman of God, but if they said that he was acting entirely on his own they would have the crowds to deal with. The Jerusalem mobs felt very strongly about their holy men, as only sinners can. I, having never sinned in my life, have always found them absurd.

The scribes refused to be cheated of an answer like this, and returned to their original question, saying, 'John did nothing against the Law, but you have brought strife to the temple of God. Is it true, then, that you can show us no sign to justify your behaviour?'

He answered them with a curse from the prophets:

I shall make the sun set at midday
    And send darkness at noon.
I shall make mourning of your feast days
    And weeping of all your songs;
I shall see you dressed in sackcloth
    And your heads I shall shave.
I shall make you weep as for an only child,
    And all your days shall be bitterness.

Many of the followers were astonished by these harsh words, and asked among themselves, 'Is this the man who comes to reconcile us with our God? Is this the Prince of Peace?' but Jesus heard them and replied,

There is a season for everything
>   And a right time for all things:
A time for loving,
>   And a time for hating,
A time for building,
>   And a time for destroying,
A time for blessing,
>   And a time for cursing,
A time for laughter,
>   And a time for tears,
A time for patience,
>   And a time for wrath,
A time for faith,
>   And a time for disgust,
A time for saviours
>   And a time for slaves,
A time for prophets
>   And a time for corpses.

With this, the priests and scribes left him; for them, this was not the time for prophets.

Jesus continued speaking to the crowd in the temple courtyard. 'Am I the Prince of Peace? I have come not to bring peace, but a sword. I have come to set father against son and mother against daughter. I will turn husband against wife and brother against brother, and I will not cease my work until the harvest is complete. When the threshing is done, and the grain is safe in the storehouse, and the chaff has been scattered by the wind and burned, then there will be time for peace.'

Followers asked him, 'Who is the grain and who is the chaff?' and 'When will these things happen?' and Jesus replied, 'These things must come to pass at their appointed time, but that is not for you to know. There will be wars and uprisings, massacres and slaughter. Do not be alarmed: the grain will be stored safely away, and the chaff will be subjected to the flames. You yourselves will be dragged before the courts to bear witness to my name. You will be flogged and scourged, your eyes will be put out and your skin peeled off in strips, your limbs will be split like kindling and your guts torn out and left to the flies. Do not fear those who can do these things to your body and then can do no more: no, fear him whose word sends you to heaven or to hell. I am the son of that great father. I shall sit at his right hand on that final day, and you will pass before me, and I will pass judgement on you, and the judgement I pass will be written with flames in the great book. Some of you who are here with me today will say to me, "Lord, I was there with you in the temple, I cast out demons in your name, I was your brother, save me", and I will say to them, "I never knew you." Others will pass before me and I will say, "You offered a cool drink to a child with no thought of reward: for this I welcome you into paradise."'

Some of the followers asked again, 'How can we know if we are the grain or the chaff?' and my brother replied, 'With the measure you use, so it will be measured to you. Good works are the surest way to life.'

The crowd seemed hopeful for a moment, and asked, 'Then good works can get us into paradise?' but Jesus replied, 'Can the chaff by striving become grain? You are what you are, and the harvester knows your hearts, though you yourselves cannot know your own hearts.'

10. This piece of bread

When the elders heard the things Jesus was saying, they wanted to remove him from the temple, but they could not, for there were many who hung on his every word.

One who was greatly moved by the way he spoke was an elder called Nicodemus, a wealthy man and well respected. There was much he wanted to discuss with Jesus, and since it was the night of the Passover meal, he invited a small group of us to share the lamb at his house.

As we were at the table, Jesus knew that this was the last time we would all eat together, and he was filled with grief and said to us, 'Remember me, my friends. Whenever you are eating and drinking together, remember me', and we were filled with a sense of doom as well. For someone who trumpeted his uniqueness and his solitary mission so relentlessly, he hated to suffer alone. Without the crowds to buoy him up with their naive questions and their shock, he was a small and lonely thing: a piece of meat still breathing, a heart loosely wrapped in temporary flesh.

Seeing his grief, and knowing that an end was near, Mary took out a jar of expensive ointment and anointed him with it, pouring it on his naked feet and on his head, covering his head with kisses and his feet with tears, and the room was filled with the perfume.

Nicodemus, sensing a hunger and a sensuality which he did not understand, became furious and began to object to the waste, suggesting that the perfume could have been sold and the money given to the poor.

Before Jesus had a chance to defend his love of luxury and his need for attention, I started ranting back at our host, saying, 'We are the poor, you fool. Who is there that we can give charity to? Rich men fast to rest their stomachs from rich food, but we don't need to fast, for we have hunger to spare. We have no cause to play at hardship.'

Then Jesus joined in, trying to wrestle a theological significance from an act of physical desire: 'Whenever this story is told, Mary's part in it will not be left out, and what she has done for me will not be forgotten.'

What he said was true: every time I have told this story, Mary's role has been my focus. What was her role? She warmed his lifeless bones and bitter heart with her humanity, but even she could not bring him to life. He was not one of us.

Then, turning to the rest of us, he said, 'In times to come, the world will recognise us by our love for one another, yet in truth I tell you that one of you is my betrayer: one whose hand is with mine on the table.'

Each of the others said to him, 'Surely you are not thinking of me', but he said nothing.

I didn't bother asking: I had had enough of such slurs already.

Now Mary was reclining next to Jesus at the table, leaning back against his chest, and she asked him who he meant, and he said to her, 'It is the one to whom I give this piece of bread.'

What I saw was this: he dipped the bread in oil and gave it to Simon, the one he had named Peter, the stumbling block.

The silly old fisherman puffed out his chest and declared, 'I will never desert you, my Lord. Even though the road take me to death, I will never fall away', but Jesus shook his head and replied, 'No, Peter, it is not your courage that I doubt. I said you would betray me, not desert me. Your road will lead to death, my friend, and you will look back over the lies you have told in my name and weep for your soul.'

Simon Peter hung his head: he had always regarded himself as the truest of my brother's followers, but he had never learned to think for himself where he was going. Without my brother he had to find his own way, and of course it was a different one. Jesus's death shocked him. He wanted it to have a meaning, a direction. He craved a new religion, new rules, new uniforms, when all there was was randomness and desire. He felt the need to create order where there was none, reason where there was none, purpose where there was none. He sought creation where there was only destruction, life where there was only death, love where there was only God. I can think of no more offensive idea than his Good News: that this vicious, pointless murder, which each of us felt as an injury to our own body, was somehow necessary, somehow preordained, somehow part of the design of the universe, part of some grand plan. Should you not regret the brutal extermination of your friend? Are you to rejoice that some callous god has chosen your brother Jesus to bear the sins of the world? To leap for joy and praise this god of wood and nails for the great honour of seeing him broken and wasted for some absurd, vindictive salvation? Who wants to live in a universe shaped by such a horror? Who wants to worship cruelty and pain? Who wants death put on a pedestal to be bowed down to and revered? Who can choose to worship the god who bound Isaac and tortured Job?

That is what I saw, but when I opened my eyes there was a piece of bread, dripping oil, on the table in front of me.

Then Jesus took bread and broke it, saying, 'This is my body, given for you: take it, draw strength from it, be filled', and Mary, drunk from the perfume, put her mouth close to his ear and spoke softly to him, saying, 'Is it true, my Lord? Your body given for me? Why is this night different from all other nights?'

Jesus lifted his eyes to the night sky and prayed that, if it could be so, he would not have to face this hour of temptation.

'Jesus, my lover,' said Mary, 'deny me no longer what my heart and body desire. Did you not say to us that your Father would answer our prayers? Then ask, my Lord, and you know you will receive. Seek, my Lord, and you know what you will find. Knock, my Lord, and you will find the door open. Despite your neglect, the chamber is warm and waiting for you to enter. Why do you wait out in the cold?'

But Jesus threw himself on the floor and prayed loudly, saying, 'Father, nothing is beyond your power. If it is your will, take this vessel from me.'

Mary was angry at the way he spoke of her, and she knelt beside him and asked, 'Do you not have the strength to sleep with me for just one hour?' Then she lifted up his robe and exposed his flesh, which lay like a dead fish, and she lamented, 'Alas, alas, my spirit is willing, but your flesh is weak.'

Then my brother pushed her away and stood up, saying, 'Do not touch me, Mary. Have you forgotten who I am? Do you think I am nothing but a man?'

'Not even so much as that,' Mary replied. 'Can this Messiah truly be the son of David? Did our great king fall so far short of manhood? Not for a second. Can beasts like us be saved by this holy ghost who is so afraid of his own flesh? You love to be slapped, my Lord, but when I offer you a kiss you do not dare to turn the other cheek.'

'My soul grieves,' said Jesus, 'and I am filled with such sorrow that this hour has come.' Then he poured a cup of wine and said, 'Drink from this, all of you. This is my blood: a new covenant. My blood poured out for the sins of those who have shared my bread.'

Mary struck the cup from his fist, spilling the wine on the floor, and ran out of the room, crying and furious.

Then Jesus turned to me and said, 'Brother, go quickly: do what you must do.'

11. What I have written

I found Mary walking the streets, muttering, clenching and unclenching her fists, cursing. I called her name, and although she almost broke stride, she neither turned nor slowed down. It was the right name, but the wrong voice. I ran and caught up with her, putting my hand on her shoulder – something I had not dared to do during my months of mute suffering – and she span around and took a swing at me. She glared at me with wildcat eyes, barely recognisable as herself under such fury, then grabbed my hand and dragged me along the streets, answering my questions with incoherent monosyllables of rage. She led me through the gates and into the garden of Gethsemane, where we – the group – had sometimes met before. And there, in a dark corner beneath some trees, she offered me everything and nothing. Nothing, because once again I was standing in for my brother, and I wanted her to make love to me: to kiss me and to say my name. Everything, because she was the universe: she was a pearl beyond price, a great treasure found buried in a field. She was all the lovers of history. She was Eve while I discovered all the sins of my newly mortal flesh. She was Rachel as I harvested seven years of toil. She was Helen of Troy, whose face may well have launched a thousand ships, but whose hips launched only one. Only Menelaus and Paris knew what they were fighting for: everyone else was a fool.

I had been with Mary only once, but I had watched her walking and sitting and bending and laughing for five months, so I knew exactly what I was missing, and I have not forgotten a single breath, a single detail. In my memory I still kiss her head, her mouth, her ear lobes, her throat, her shoulders, then down over her breasts, her sides, her belly with its lovely little mound of fat, her navel, her hips. But that is my memory, and those details are mine, and anyway, there are no words for things like that. Words are for gravity and duty, for identity and consequence. Words are for explaining that it was then that Jesus found us, lying in each other's arms beneath the trees, the air filled with ripeness and sweetness and sweat.

He looked at us bitterly, lying naked there, and I could see in my triumph how hurt he was that the woman he loved had chosen not to follow his way, and that his brother had taken the place he had denied himself.

He asked, 'Judas, my brother, do you betray me with a kiss?' and in my arrogance I replied, 'Yes, my Lord, among other things.' I accepted then the charge I now deny. I did not betray my brother: I honoured myself.

Then Jesus rebuked Mary, saying, 'Have you no shame? Do you not recall that I cast out of you seven demons?' and she replied 'Yes, my Lord, I remember well, but you refused to cast into me even one: even that one I most desired. Well, I am afraid that the seven you cast out found no other place to dwell, and they have returned to their former home, found it swept and clean, and brought your brother with them.'

Mary drew herself off me and stood up, naked, and Jesus recoiled from the sacred shock of her flesh, her curves, her skin, her twists of secret hair. She took her dress and dropped it over her raised, breast-exalting arms, leaving only her deep eyes and her inky, silky torrent of hair to tempt the son of God. 'My friend,' she continued, 'I gave up a lucrative profession to follow you.'

'Friend?' he snapped. 'You are my friend if you do what I tell you. You have offered me no more than was my due. From the one who has been forgiven much, much is expected.'

'Is this the ground on which you choose to reproach me?' Mary cried. 'What more could you expect? No one has loved you as I have.'

'Indeed, my sweet child, indeed,' said Jesus, 'I cannot even permit you to love me as you do.'

'Then why have I followed you, if not to love you?' she asked. 'You are the vine, and we are your branches, yet you do not even dare to taste the fruit which hangs upon your sweetest limb. What good has it done you to abstain from the God-created pleasures of my bed, only to stew in your own skin?'

She tried to take hold of him, but he repulsed her, saying, 'Do not cling to me, Mary.'

I stood behind her and tried to put my arms around her to comfort her, to bring her close to me, to help myself believe that what we had done was a real, solid, trustworthy thing, but it was not me that she wanted, and I too was left with empty arms.

Jesus turned to his companions and asked, 'What is to become of a woman taken in the act of adultery? What does the law say?'

'She is to be put to death, my Lord,' said Simon. He had left his wife in Galilee to follow his Messiah and become a fisher of men, but he had learned little of compassion on the way. A shepherd of men could perhaps have understood gentleness, patience, kindness and forgiveness, but a fisherman never meets his fish without killing them.

I replied, 'Yes, Peter, but let the one who is without sin cast the first stone,' and this time Mary consented to find a little shelter in my arms.

Jesus withdrew a little way from us and stooped to write in the dust on the ground. After a short while he looked up and saw his followers standing, watching him. Looking from one to the other he asked, 'Have none of us the courage to obey the law? Is this sin, and are these stones, and not one of us has the strength to pick them up? Then the time has come for the son of man to learn of suffering.'

With those words, Jesus set off for Jerusalem. We looked at what he had drawn in the dust, and saw a man hanging on a cross, and the words 'My God, my God, why have you forsaken me?'

Simon called after Jesus, asking, 'What is this that you have drawn in the dust, my Lord?' and his Messiah replied to him, 'What I have written, I have written.'

12. One thing that bothers me still

In the end was the word.
Call it by any name, in any language;
    Spell it however you like –
        Crucifix, tomb, suicide, corpse –
    It is always the same word.
In the end he was dead,
    And we were left behind,
    And it wasn't fun any more,
    And everywhere was ugliness.
In the end was the word,
    And the word was not God,
    And the word was not with God,
    And God was nowhere to be found.
The word was death,
    And we found ourselves in its shadow,
    And we found it biting our heel
    And we found it within ourselves,
        Where once we had found laughter and joy
        And companionship and desire.
Can language express a doubt so deep?
So many words for things we hated:
    No words good enough
    For the things we loved.

I am an old man now, far older than is necessary: older, perhaps, than is even excusable. I have outlived my friends and am writing this book to keep myself company, to preserve the stories that now cannot be told. They killed him in the end, but we lived on. Now my beloved

Mary joins the dead, and even the end is drawing to a close. After this is nothing, but I am not afraid. Lonely, yes, and tired, but not afraid. I have lived so many years past my time that not existing will be quite a relief.

Apart from those few months of my youth, I can barely recall the details of a single day. We suffered the curse of having been in the right place at the right time, of living through a moment so intense that nothing could ever equal it. I suffered most, by which I mean I suffered longest.

Would it have been different had he lived? Perhaps, perhaps, had he not sought to die. He courted death in those months, daring it to claim him, seeking something within its arms that he could not find among us. The thought of it helped him through many a lonely night. Often he spoke of his death as something to be aspired to, or as another man might speak of his wife, as of a companion with whom he longed to be reunited. He told us that he would send us a spirit, a comforter who would never leave us, but it seems that few of us shared his idea of comfort. We did not choose to wrap ourselves in oblivion as we lay down to sleep; the void bundled up beneath our heads for a pillow.

He was a bitter, evil man, my brother. His desire was not to enlighten. Perhaps he imagined that in public death lay fame and immortality, but he will never know what is being done in his name, or how immortality more than anything else has obscured his uniqueness. He is remembered chiefly for things he didn't say, and for one event that was not in his control. No one remembers his wit, his scurrilous sense of humour, his earthiness, his self-doubt, his loneliness, his desperate need for a woman's kiss to revive his belief in himself.

Can you imagine him grown old, as we who were left grew old? To be a faded man recalling former days when anything seemed possible: a new miracle, a new curse, an original sin? If he hadn't died when he did, he would never have lived it down. He was lucky: death suited him. That moment which contained the whole world contained also its destruction: he was like Sodom, consumed in the flower of its glory.

Looking back, my life has been a pillar of salt, but now that salt has lost its flavour and is fit only to be thrown in the street and trampled underfoot.

Though there is one thing that bothers me still: one question left inadequately answered. There was a man who had two sons; there were two brothers; there were two men and a woman. You know the story. There was a man who loved a woman, but she loved his brother, but the brother died, and then she loved him. There was a woman who loved a man, but he died, and then she loved his brother. There was a man who loved a woman, and before he died strangers came to him with questions.

They said, 'There was a man who had two sons. The first was married to a woman, but he died leaving no children, so his brother married her, as is the custom, but he too gave her no children. Eventually she died, and finally the brother too must die, a lonely old man mourning his love and his youth. Since both were married to her, who will be her husband at the resurrection?'

To which he replied, 'My body is not yet cold and you are marrying off my widow. Kill me first, and then I will answer your question.'

It is the only story there is, ever since God looked with favour on Abel and not on Cain: Jacob have I loved, Esau have I hated; Ishmael is sent out into the desert, while Isaac becomes the heir; Solomon's older brother must die before he can be born to rule. The firstborn dies, the second inherits: he should not have been surprised. Inherits what? I never thought to ask.

Who will be her husband now, Jesus? You, who she loved in those whirlwind days when the world seemed too small for our desires? Or me, her partner for these last slow years, these forty years in the wilderness, this lifetime waiting for death to realise its mistake and collect its debts?

I can answer the question now: there is no resurrection; this is all we have. And now that I have had all there is to have, I wonder at the smallness of it.

Would it have been better if there was a god? We cured ourselves of faith, but not of yearning. Who am I to thank for rain, for the sunset, for dates and figs? Who am I to praise for that moment when I am making love with my wife and my body fits hers so perfectly that the whole world seems tender and safe and welcoming? There is no one. Who do I blame when my child falls ill and dies, and no one has the faintest idea why? Who do I hold responsible when locusts strip every leaf from my olive trees and leave them a naked grove of obscene gestures? And who do I curse when I am in love with a woman and she is in love with my brother? Nothing.

We were right: there was no future. I had hoped we were wrong.